JAGGED EDGES

SHANNON S. LESANE

DEDICATION

To my beloved daughter, never set limits on your dreams,
your voice, or your light.

CONTENTS

ACKNOWLEDGMENTS

Thank you to my family, who always believed in me, even when I didn't believe in myself. Your unwavering love, encouragement, and faith have carried me through the moments when I doubted my voice and my worth. This book would not exist without the foundation of your support, and for that, I am forever grateful.

A LETTER TO MY DAUGHTER
March 2025

Dear Beloved,

Hopefully, I've told you this often enough, but I am so proud of the young woman you have become.

After you shared the news about the baby last Sunday, so many emotions overwhelmed me. I immediately became concerned about your health. Fear, anxiety, and panic seemed to wash over me all at once. I wondered if you would be okay, if the baby would be okay. I wondered if you were in the right place—physically and emotionally—to go through a pregnancy right now.

But you assured your Dad and me that you were fine, and that the baby was fine. You mentioned all the prenatal tests you've taken and that most of them had already come back with good results.

And I couldn't have been more stunned as I looked at the ultrasound — that perfectly shaped head and little nose... I just knew then it was a boy. I remember finally managing to say the word "Congratulations" and coming over to hug you. I didn't want to hurt you with my delayed reaction. I wanted you to know that I love you, and that you have my full support.

Later, my thoughts began to wander to the man you've chosen to have this baby with. I wondered if this was the right choice for you, but I quickly realized that it's your life, your decision. I know you're both still

1

figuring things out, and though you're young, I trust that you're thinking this through carefully.

I'm not worried about you making the right decision, but I just want you to feel truly loved and supported every step of the way.

You know that I believe in the commitment of marriage, and I believe that love and devotion should always be the foundation of any relationship. But I want to emphasize that I will always respect your choices, and I don't want you to feel pressured by anything I've said. I just want you to feel that you've found a love that will be enduring, faithful, and true — whether it's now or later.

After all these years of talking about your wedding and someday having children, I never imagined this would be how it would happen. In fact, you used to say to me that having kids would be a long, long time from now — or even, "I don't really think about that. I don't wonder about weddings."

Yet here you are, in less than two years, in love and expecting your first child.

After spending days thinking about you and this baby, and hardly *anything else, I decided to do something with my emotions. Anytime I've felt such intense feelings in the past, I've turned to writing. One night, I dreamed about writing you a letter, and the next day I found my old notebook filled with poems and writings I've saved over the years.*

Today, I finally sat down to write some of the words I've been carrying around, and it became a poem — "Are You Happy?" As the day went on, I gathered other poems and vignettes and decided to gift them to you and my grandson.

Although we are two very different people, I think you may have some of the same feelings I had in my early twenties. Maybe you can relate to some of my writings. Maybe not. But something tells me that my grandson may someday find interest in them.

Wouldn't it be something if he grew up to be a famous author? Believe it or not, I can already see and feel him now. I know he is meant to be here. God makes no mistakes.

I'm looking forward to his arrival. It almost feels like I've been waiting for him all this time.

I love you so much, Jellybean. You couldn't make me prouder. I support you, and I will always have your back — even beyond the grave. That means for eternity.

With all my love,

Mommy

A LETTER TO FUTURE SON-IN-LAW

2025

Dear Future Son-in-Law,

My mind has been in overdrive since you both shared the news about the baby. As you well know, our daughter means the world to us. Not only is she our only daughter, whom we love deeply, but she is also an amazing human being. She is the kindest, gentlest person I know - the kind of person who may give more of herself than she should.

Since coming into this world, things have not always been easy for her, yet I've heard her say at times that she has had it easy for most of her life. I mean, she has never been stung by a bee! I chuckle at this because it's actually something she once told me, and I couldn't believe that, out of all the things she may have experienced at this point in her life, being stung by a bee, in her mind, would be the worst.

When our daughter first met you, there was something different about her. She is of a quiet nature and does not always share what she is thinking or feeling. But there was confidence in the way she talked about you that I had never seen before. I asked her one day what was so different about you. She replied that you don't keep her guessing. You tell her how you are feeling and what you are thinking, and she doesn't have to wonder. I remember thinking for some time afterward about the kind of man you are. Who taught you this? A young man with such intent and purpose at your age is rare.

I've met your mother and father, and I can see there is so much love there for you. They are extremely proud of their sons. The Christmas before last, I took a photo of your mother with you and your brother, and I could see the pride and love all over her face. It is comforting to know that my daughter loves a man who has been shown unconditional love. There are many men and women out there who don't know what that feels like.

I want to be honest when I say that I'm not certain what kind of man you will show up to be for my daughter and grandson. Please know there is no pressure to be anyone other than who you are. I can only ask or hope that you will be patient, kind, and loyal. Please show them a love that is constant, unwavering, and accepting. Take care of yourself and take good care of them.

I know that our daughter loves you. And soon, both of you will have the hardest but most rewarding roles of your lives as parents. Look to each other for strength - you are going to need that most of all. Please know that we will always be here and will fully support you both. You are a part of the family now, and we don't take that designation lightly.

Never forget what our daughter loves about you. I ask that you continue to be a man of intent, because it's what you plant before anything grows.

Sincerely,
SSL

ARE YOU HAPPY?
2025

Are you happy,
my beloved?

I ask this question,
but something tells me the answer
is in your quiet smile—
the smile on our walks
that warms my heart
and makes me wonder
what you're thinking of.
Yet I don't ask,
so I don't interrupt your thoughts.

I want you always to be happy,
content with your choices in love and life,
never regretting a single moment—
for you deserve all things good and kind,
loving and forgiving,
protecting and enduring.

Are you happy,
my beloved?
I ask this question,
but something tells me the answer
is in your eyes,
like a mirror reflecting back at me—
my quiet knowing and your quiet smile.

No need to answer
what is already known.

A MOTHER'S WAR
1999

The message came that evening.
I stood there, motionless –
hearing, half believing.
Soon, there would be a baby,
one that I carried.
Ashamed – for shame –
I wasn't married.

Inhaling slowly,
I hung up the phone.
Exhaling, I remembered –
I wasn't alone.

The war was just beginning,
with battles I had to win.
I was responsible for this new life,
and I vowed to protect and defend.
Determined that this baby would be,
I labored for her existence
with all the strength within me.

At last, I cradled her in my arms
this tiny being –
one my heart had beat for,
giving my blood, my breath, my feelings.
I praised God that she was alive,
so grateful that we had survived.

Now, I battle the Beasts in the life of mankind.
I can no longer protect her in my womb.
She is free to experience the world –
how it can deceive and destroy a young girl.

Frantic,
I shield her from all that I can.
The Beasts will not pollute her innocence,
I say, holding her tiny hand.
I wage war, yet I am losing the battle,
wishing I had known it was more than I could handle.
The Beasts have made her ill, hurt, cry –
Beasts that I vow to fight like a soldier
until the day that I die.

I pray, God, to help me keep my vow.
I must win this wretched war –
You must show me how.

I pray, God –
show my daughter what I can't.
Wounded by this battle, I must pray.
Show her forgiveness when they betray.
Show her You can defeat
what her mother can't slay.
Give her truth when they lie.
Show her Your strength
when her mother must cry.

When they make her feel worthless,
make her see that she counts.
Give her confidence and spirit
when her mother is in doubt.

God, I am praying for Your alliance
in this war against the Beasts.
Give me Your strength and power –
please help me defeat!

MIXED EMOTIONS
2014

I am strong and fearless.
I can look you straight in the eye
and let you know what I can do for you
and what you can do for me.

I can be disappointed, but not discouraged,
because that missed opportunity was only one
of the many that will come my way.

I smile because I know the secret,
and I hold the key to my happiness.
That key is me.

I am weak and afraid.
I look away
because I cannot express how I feel
or what I need from you.

I can be grateful, yet still yearning,
because so many opportunities come my way,
but I let them slip away.

I frown because I do not know the secret,
and I am unable to find the key to my happiness—
that key that is never me.

OUR LOVE IS POETIC RHYTHM
1995

When we are together
Our love is like the rhythm
of sweet poetry.
Each beat unfettered,
our hearts beat a love song
in our moments of passion
that no one can understand.
Its words so undefined
that only you and I can comprehend.
With each sensual beat,
we are lost in an intoxicating verse
that only we know the words –
Our voices echoing the sounds
of this erotic song that resounds
throughout our bodies.

HER LETTER TO GOD
1997

I am writing a letter to God.
And in this letter,
I am praying for an answer—
on how to get my life together.

At times, my life seems so rough,
and there are so many moments
when I just want to give up.

I am asking for God's forgiveness
for any wrongs that I have done,
and to have mercy on me
if I have ever hurt someone.

I've known for some time
that I wouldn't make it like this—
always putting God last
and my wants first on my list.

There were times I was always needing
and never receiving,
wanting more—
always searching and never finding,
always looking up but never climbing.

Through it all, God has been my friend.
When I feared and couldn't sleep,
He put my fears to an end.
When I was so lonely,

He sent me someone to love—
and even then, I needed more,
because love wasn't enough.

He gave me a child
when I felt I wasn't ready,
knowing all the while
her love would keep me steady.

God has always blessed me
with what I needed,
made me realize
what I couldn't see.

So, as I sit here in tears,
writing this letter,
I feel so torn up inside,
asking that He'll make it better.

Hoping that He'll help me understand
why the love He blessed me with
seems to be coming to an end.

Praying that I can go on with my life,
accomplishing something more than
mother, lover, friend, and wife.

I am writing this letter to God,
and in this letter,
I am praying for an answer.

HIS FORGIVENESS
1999

He had to forgive her –
She was the mother of his children.
She was there when he felt he had no one.
She believed that he was someone more
that he felt he could ever be.
She told him that he would succeed,
and he did.

He forgave her –
It wasn't her fault that she gave in.
Not everyone could be strong –
Some are just weak,
some just give up.

She made a promise
He knew she could never keep,
But he forgives her for that too.
She made this promise after
he had kneeled before her bedside
and cried into her hands-
His salty tears soaking her in his grief

He feels so empty – unsatisfied,
Afraid to search deeply within himself
to find what is missing.
He is afraid he may realize
that his emptiness goes far beyond
the reality that she has left him,

and that he has not really
forgiven her at all.

I FORGIVE YOU
1999

Sit down and listen to me,
For once I have something to say.
Sit down.
I want you to hear what I'm feeling.
I've kept it inside for so long.
You wouldn't listen before,
but you will listen today.

I want to tell you that
You have hurt me,
deceived me, turned your back on me.
You never believed in me,
You have betrayed me,
You made me feel
less
      than
         a human being.
I see you're trying to walk away,
But I won't let you –
Today you will listen.
You will not cover your ears –
Not hearing,
Denying
What you have done to me.
I want you to see that
Even though you tried to destroy me,
I still survived.
Don't tell me you never knew!

The words never crossed my lips,
but you saw what you were doing to me
by the way my head hung low,
shoulders slumped – weak from
hurting, begging, and praying.
But now you see the woman I am today –
My shoulders are stronger now.
I can carry the weight of the past,
but I will not succumb to its misery.
I will not let it destroy me!

So today you will listen
to the strong, self-confident, beautiful woman
that you have created.
No longer the weak, distraught little girl
begging for your forgiveness.
Today, I want you to finally hear me –
I want you to know that
I
Forgive
You.

MOTHER'S KITCHEN
1999

I walk into a silent house. Instantly, I feel a warmth that can only come from being home and around things familiar. I quietly close the door so as not to disturb the silence of the living room. I inhale deeply, taking in the delicious aroma of something simmering from the kitchen. The savory smell of sage beckons me closer to the kitchen, searching for whatever it is my mother is cooking.

I walk into the small, cozy kitchen. A soft breeze is blowing through the half-cracked window by the refrigerator. The bright yellow curtains flutter playfully against the windowsill. My mother always complains about how hot it gets when she is cooking, so it's no surprise that the window is open in the middle of winter. I lean against the refrigerator, which is one of the new appliances in the kitchen with its blinding bright white color. Very soon, I won't have to stand on my tiptoes to reach a box of cereal or anything else, which is stored on top of the refrigerator when there is no room in the cabinets.

My mother is silently standing by the sink. She is wearing a brightly colored, striped dress she often wears around the house. The water is spouting from the sink as she is washing dishes slowly, with suds covering one side of the sink. My mother's arms are halfway covered in suds, as she hasn't noticed that I'm here. I wait patiently as my eyes roam to the simmering pot on the stove. My mother is preparing her famous stewed chicken and rice. I call it famous because it's my favorite, and it should be famous as far as I'm concerned.

I notice how old the pot is, missing one handle, and the lid where the white paint has worn away. My mother says she had the pots long before I was born, and they are still in good condition. Even the old white stove has been here longer than I have, with some burners not working. My mother can only use two burners at a time while she is cooking, so her meals are paced, and it usually takes a while for dinner to be ready, especially on Sundays.

I notice how dim the kitchen is, with only the slowly fading light of the afternoon sun flowing in from the window. I shuffle my feet against the hardwood floor of the kitchen. I always wonder why there's no tile on the floor like the kitchens in my friends' houses, but I decide I'll never ask my mother why. I grab my stomach as it grumbles noisily. I can't wait until she finishes cooking.

YELLOW BIRD
2023

Yesterday, I was sitting on the back porch, chatting with my daughter, when I saw a bright yellow and black bird fluttering nearby. It landed on a lawn chair just as I pointed it out to her. Together, we watched it flutter to the ground and then take off toward the garden. A quick search identified the bird as an *American Goldfinch*.

My daughter grinned as the finch began to chirp in the distance — a lively, energetic sound. Yet, as I listened, I suddenly felt a wave of sadness.

The bird reminded me of my late Aunt Brenda, one of several family members we've lost in the past couple of years. She once shared a story about red birds and their spiritual connection to loved ones who have passed on. One morning, shortly after her son tragically died, her backyard filled with red birds. She found comfort in their presence, believing it was her son's way of letting her know all was well.

Thinking of her story, I wondered if yellow birds held some kind of spiritual symbolism too. A quick search revealed that the goldfinch is associated with *celebration, joy, and good things to come*. I read those words over and over again: *Celebration. Joy. Good things to come.*

Like many, I've found it difficult over the past few years to gather, celebrate, or not worry about what's ahead. The uncertainty of the pandemic, life changes, loss, and other challenges have made it hard to feel joyful or hopeful, let alone

celebratory. But through it all, I've remained grateful. And recently, I've been fortunate enough to gather with family and, dare I say, feel a bit of joy — though that gathering did not come without risk.

Maybe it's just a coincidence. But maybe that little yellow bird fluttered by to remind me — and anyone else who needs to hear it — that even amid challenges, painful setbacks, and loss, we must find our way back to joy. Life is meant to be lived, even when it comes with risks.

So, for anyone needing a little extra encouragement today: take the chance, accept the offer, go on the trip, forgive yourself. Do what brings you joy.

Good things *are* to come.

IT'S GOOD TO KNOW YOU
1999

It was good getting to know you,
and now we are forever connected.
I enjoyed our talks
and spending time with you.

Such a short time we've spent
in each other's presence,
but we have found we have a lot in common.
It feels like we've known each other
long before we met.

And now it's time for you to go.
I question why we ever met.
Perhaps it was fate
that we did.
We've learned from each other,
and we have grown to understand
ourselves better by sharing common experiences.

I am glad to have met you,
and someday our paths will meet again.
And at that time,
we will remember the people we used to be.
Maybe we will laugh
at some of our own stories,
and it will be like we never parted.

We have planted a seed
that, over the years,

I hope it continues to grow and flourish.
In our short time,
it was so good getting to know you—
and now, forever.

SIBLING RIVALRY
ABT. 2005

A thought suddenly came to me
how we were as children.
We shared everything—
laughs, fears, secrets, clothes.
Even our opinions were the same.

Do you remember how we used to take care of each other?
How we created trails to imaginary cities
in a world all our own?

We created a society of honor and loyalty.
The sibling bond was so great.

Yet today, after time has worn on,
the lights have dimmed,
the buildings have crumbled,
and the key to the city is lost.

I miss the adventures,
the less complicated life
of childhood.
It was then we could dream up fantastical cities,
where we were kings and queens,
where our love and respect for each other ruled.
It was a time when we did not fear,
we never looked back,
we forgave and forgot,
and we realized the value of brother and sister.

What could break a bond so strong?
What could destroy a city and leave it in ruins?
How do we get back there?
How do we rebuild?
Is it even possible, now that
we have families of our own,
where we must dream and build our own worlds around
them?

Is it possible, or did our fantastical city ever exist?
Will we someday again find the keys
to the now crumbled city?

ALONE
2015

John poured coffee down his throat as if it would wash away his sins from the night before. His breath stank of too much alcohol, and the odor made his stomach queasy. He looked up at the clock and instantly grabbed his head. The simple motion sent throbbing pains throughout his temples. It was 6:00 a.m. He had just come home three hours ago and was relieved she wasn't there. She wouldn't approve — and those eyes — the accusations, the disappointment that would be there. He couldn't bear it, not now, not today.

John stood slowly and made his way over to the pantry. He winced as he bent over, frantically searching the large storage container on the floor. He forced his arm through the junk stacked inside the container. He moved it all out of the way: folded tablecloths, boxes of trash bags, old plastic bags, matches, candles. He pushed, pulled, shifted, and then he grabbed what he was looking for, all the way at the bottom. He pulled out the small glass bottle, satisfied, being careful not to smile too wide. He feared the act would split his skull in two.

John removed the top of the bottle and emptied its contents into the coffee mug. *She wouldn't approve,* he thought as he drank the coffee with new gusto. He stuffed the evidence of his bad behavior deep within his pocket. He didn't know why he bothered. She wouldn't be back. He suddenly felt tired, his shoulders heavy. There it was again, that feeling that made it difficult to move and constricted his breathing. He sat at the kitchen table. *She would never come back,* and there wasn't a thing he could do about it.

John leaned over with his face in his hands. He welcomed the darkness there. He suddenly became aware of how empty the room felt. He could hear himself breathing and the appliances in the kitchen humming in the background. He could smell stale cigarette smoke and perfume in his clothes. He began to tap his foot gently against the base of the kitchen table. He told himself she was only in the next room, sleeping. *Maybe she had changed her mind.* All he had to do was wash his face and brush his teeth. *She was waiting for him.*

Energized for a moment by the thought of her being there, John felt his heart beat rapidly against his chest. He stood from the table and staggered his way to the next room. The door to the bedroom was closed, and he stood there staring for a moment, not breathing, as he placed his ear against the door. The wood felt cool against the rough stubble of his jaw. He could hear nothing. He reached for the doorknob and slowly turned.

The door of the bedroom swung open as John stood there expectantly, unmoving, as the full room came into view. He was pained to find it just as he had left it. The bed was unmade, the covers thrown to the side where she would have been sleeping. His shoes and clothes were scattered about the room, with a bath towel he used yesterday evening left at the foot of the bed. She would hate that. She would nag him to put it away.

John walked into the room and stood at the edge of the empty bed. That feeling was back. This time he wouldn't fight it. It started at the pit of his stomach and began to move upward.

When it reached his chest and he could not breathe, he fell to the edge of the bed. He tried to hold on, but his arms and legs were numb from the feelings taking over him. He fell to the floor. The feeling slowly spread upward to his throat. He tried to speak, but there were no words, and his mouth remained open in shock as the flushed feeling took over his face and his eyes began to water.

He shuddered violently and squeezed his eyes shut. He could not stop the tears as they flowed for the first time since she left. He had never felt so alone and empty — and welcomed death. *Surely, he was dying.* He was tired of missing her, needing her, wanting her...

John lay there in his feelings of guilt, regret, and emptiness. He loved her, and he hated her. She had left him. It was his fault. She was never coming back, and there was nothing he could do about it.

WHAT TIME IS IT?
2013

"What time is it?" Harold glanced at his watch, then looked at his wife in exasperation.

"12:45 p.m.," his wife Miriam responded, not looking up from her magazine.

"We've been waiting thirty-five minutes to see the doctor!" Harold pointed to his watch in disbelief. He paused as the nurse walked into the waiting room and a young couple sat in the chairs nearby. He tried his best to smile in greeting, but he was too annoyed to be friendly at the moment.

"I've never waited this long at the other hospital," he said, repositioning himself in his chair. He smoothed away imaginary wrinkles from his trousers. Miriam had just starched his pants the night before; there were no wrinkles in sight. "You know, I had my surgery on the 14th, and they said they were—"

"I know, Harold," Miriam interjected. "I'm gonna tell 'em. They were supposed to call us two weeks after the surgery, but we ain't heard nothing from 'em." She shook her head, her tight brown curls bouncing. She had spent all day last Saturday getting her hair washed and set. She hoped it wasn't raining when they left. She saw the clouds on their drive in, and her head was aching something awful — a sure sign rain was on the way.

Harold watched as Miriam flipped the page of her magazine. He noticed her neatly manicured nails. Today, Miriam was wearing a funny-looking clear polish that looked like pearls. That was probably where she was last Saturday when he called her several times, and she didn't pick up. God forbid Miriam mess up her nails. Never mind that he had just choked on a chicken bone and barely lived to tell it if the nurse hadn't been there. He noted Miriam's flowery green dress and her tan loafers. Were those new? He thought of an earlier discussion they'd had on the way to the clinic.

"So Johnny Pickens is writing a book?" he asked.

"No, he already wrote the book. That's what Mary said in church on Sunday." Miriam flipped another page of her magazine. Harold furrowed his brow, trying to think hard. He knew two or three Marys. Which one was it?

Harold ran his hand through his salt-and-pepper hair and repositioned his bifocals. "Well, who the hell is Johnny Pickens anyway?" He stood up to leave.

"That's Lula Mae's boy. You know Lula who took over Macon's grocery—" Miriam looked up to see her husband disappear behind the bathroom door near the waiting area. She shook her head and pursed her lips. He was always doing that.

A few minutes later, Harold reappeared. He began to walk over but then stopped mid-stride. He gripped his stomach.

"What's wrong with you?" Miriam asked, slightly alarmed.

"It's just gas," Harold responded, as he passed gas loudly in the open, quiet space of the waiting area.

The couple who sat nearby bowed their heads in quiet laughter.

"Sorry, y'all," Harold apologized to the couple. "I'll sit over here in case more slips out." He sat near the bathroom door and looked at his watch.

"It's been forty-five minutes," he said, pointing at his watch again. "Come on, doctor, I ain't got all day."

"We have all day," Miriam said, setting her magazine aside and crossing her arms. She smiled at the couple as if to apologize for her husband's rude behavior.

"You wanna sit here in this chair all day?" Harold didn't pause for Miriam's response. "I got better things to do."

"We ain't got nothin' to do, Harold. Might as well wait."

"Is everyone all right?" The nurse asked, coming into the waiting area. She smiled politely at the waiting patients.

"Yes, ma'am, we're all right," Miriam smiled back.

"I ain't all right," Harold folded his arms and sat back in his chair. "We've been waitin' forty-five minutes."

"I am so sorry. Dr. Preminger is running a little behind today," the nurse smiled again. "Can I get you anything while you wait?"

"I need to see the doctor." Harold got up from his chair and walked over to the nurse. He squinted his eyes as he read her name tag. "Ms. Brown, y'all have too many patients. You need to get some help. I never had to wait this long at the other hospital."

Nurse Brown listened patiently as Harold went on.

"You know I had my surgery on the 14th, and no one called to follow up. I'm just coming in today, and it's two months later.

When my wife had her surgery at the other hospital, the doctor gave us his home number and everything. He treated her like his own mama. Y'all were supposed to call weeks ago. You didn't, and that ain't right."

"I am so sorry about that, Mr. Stalinger. Thank you for sharing that with me. That is not a usual occurrence. All of our patients are contacted within two weeks post-op. We'll need to find out what went wrong." Nurse Brown was apologetic, and she seemed sincere enough to Harold.

"Yes, well, I guess I feel all right anyway." Harold relaxed as he realized he had a sympathetic ear. "I thought I was never gonna use the bathroom right again, but Dr. Preminger hooked me right up. I got a bag here in front and one in back. One for each kidney." Harold pointed to where the drainage bags were located underneath his shirt.

"Harold?" Miriam interrupted. "Everybody doesn't need to know that. Come on over here and sit down and leave Nurse Brown alone."

"Well, hell, Miriam, everybody knows this is a urology clinic. Ain't no shame or surprise I had kidney surgery." Harold frowned at his wife as she gave him "the look"—the look he knew all too well, that he had gone too far. He decided he would continue his friendly chat with Nurse Brown. Miriam would be all right once they got in to see the doctor.

"You know I got the prettiest little pull-ups too," he said, smiling at Nurse Brown.

"Oh!" Nurse Brown said, trying not to smile.

"Harold—seriously!" Miriam was openly angry at Harold.

"She's just mad 'cause I won't let her use any of 'em," Harold chuckled to himself as the young couple also laughed, this time openly.

"Mr. Stalinger?" a voice called out from the entrance of the waiting room.

Harold looked over at the woman who had just entered the room. She was holding a clipboard and looking expectantly around the room.

"I'm Mr. Stalinger!" Harold yelled. The woman smiled in his direction.

"I'm Dr. Preminger's assistant, Sarah. I apologize he's running behind, but he is ready to see you now."

"'Bout time," Harold nodded politely to Nurse Brown, then motioned for his wife to come forward.

"Come on, Miriam. I hope Dr. Preminger hurries up with me 'cause I'm gonna need a Big Mac after this."

Miriam rolled her eyes and hurried after her husband. It would be a long day indeed.

A WALLET, 50 CENTS & NAIL
2014

"Do they have ham?" Harold scratched his head, squinting at the menu spread across the wall above the counter.

"No, this is McDonald's. They don't serve ham for lunch," Miriam responded.

"Well, I want a ham sandwich." Harold shoved his hands into his pockets. He felt around to make sure the items he had placed there earlier were still safely within.

"I just said they don't serve ham." Miriam stepped forward in the line, and Harold followed.

"What kind of place don't serve ham for lunch?" Harold shook his head. "That don't make no sense!"

"May I help you, ma'am?" The young woman across the counter smiled at Miriam and Harold as they stepped forward.

"We'll have two grilled chicken sandwiches with side salads." Miriam unzipped her purse to retrieve her wallet.

"Are you kidding me?" Harold shook his head in disbelief. "I don't eat nothing grilled, and you know it, Miriam!"

Miriam sighed as she pulled a few dollars from her wallet. "Please change that order to a grilled chicken sandwich and a ten-piece chicken nugget with BBQ sauce."

The cashier nodded, then punched the order into the register.

"Would you like drinks with that?"

"We'll have a cup of water and a Diet Pepsi," Miriam responded.

"Ok, that will be $12.00." The cashier looked up. Harold frowned.

"Mighty expensive for no ham," he mumbled. A faint smile spread across the cashier's lips, but she said nothing.

Miriam paid the cashier and stepped aside to wait for the order.

"I'm going to find a table outside." Harold didn't wait for Miriam to acknowledge him before heading for the door. Once outside, he looked around for the cleanest table he could find, then took a seat. He breathed in deeply, savoring the aroma of french fries wafting from the restaurant. He swatted at a bug as he watched a car back out of a parking space, then drive away.

It was a sunny, seventy-degree spring day. Every now and then, a breeze would float by, bringing a whiff of flowers or triggering a sneeze from the pollen. Harold reached into his pocket, pulling out his wallet. He looked up for a moment as a man and his young daughter exited McDonald's and gave him a wave. He waved back, then opened the wallet to review the contents inside. A few old business cards and some pictures of his grandchildren remained exactly where he had placed them. He stopped carrying money long ago. Miriam handled the money now. This was because, at eighty years old, Harold had a hard time keeping up with his wallet. He did, however, carry fifty cents. Remembering the fifty cents, Harold pulled the two quarters from his pocket and placed them on the table in front of him. The silver coins sparkled in the sunlight. He never left home without fifty cents in his pocket. He never knew when he might need an emergency soda pop, even if sometimes he had to ask Miriam for an additional seventy-five cents to buy one from the vending machine.

Harold placed the wallet and fifty cents back into his right pocket. He reached deep within his left pocket and pulled out a small brown nail. He brought it close to his face to inspect its wear. He had seen it in the parking lot at the doctor's office and felt very fortunate to have found it. As a matter of fact, he looked for nails in every parking lot he went to. Neither Miriam nor the kids ever understood why. They called it a weird obsession with nails, but they didn't know. They didn't understand how deadly a nail could be. Harold would never forget the Evans family and how a small nail in the tire tragically ended their lives. He'd been picking up nails since he was twelve years old and truly believed he was saving lives.

Harold looked up as Miriam sat next to him, placing the tray of food onto the table. The aroma of fried chicken engulfed his senses. He forgot about the nail for the moment and reached for the chicken nuggets.

"Stop. You've been handling that old rusty nail." Miriam cautioned. She reached into her purse. "Give me your hand." She squeezed hand sanitizer into his palm. "Now eat, it's time to take your medicine."

JAGGED EDGES
2022

I often write things down. Sometimes the notes are used as a reminder, and other times they are thoughts that eventually become something more. I scrolled through a few notes today and found the words written below. I am not sure what triggered those thoughts that day, but I think of the younger version of me and my career choices as I read over them. Indeed, not a linear path – I've landed in places I never dreamed of and lost opportunities of my dreams. I've had experiences that taught me lessons I'll never forget, and some better left forgotten. I've made life-long connections and am better for them. Although I sometimes wonder about alternative paths - safer routes that didn't expose me to certain biases, disappointment, and just plain old unkindness as I navigated my way through. I now realize the path taken was necessary. The journey made me stronger, wiser, and more appreciative of my opportunities and those yet to be discovered. I've learned to trust myself and not be afraid of the journey. Setbacks are temporary. Look back, look forward, adjust – Keep Going!

The path I took -
Jagged, some edges hurt.

ABOUT THE AUTHOR

Shannon S. Lesane is a freelance writer based in Raleigh, North Carolina, with a passion for poetry, short stories, personal essays, and reflective letters that explore the complexities of love, family, faith, and forgiveness. Through her writing, Shannon captures moments of vulnerability, resilience, and the deep ties that connect us to those we love, especially the bonds between mothers and daughters, and the lessons passed through generations.

Writing has always been Shannon's way of making sense of the world, a quiet place to explore her own experiences, struggles, and hopes. Much of her work draws on her life as a mother, daughter, wife, and woman navigating life's many jagged edges. Her poems, vignettes, and letters reflect a desire to leave behind a legacy of words — messages of love, strength, and truth for her family.

When she is not writing, Shannon enjoys reading stories that speak to the human spirit, gardening as a form of peace and reflection, and traveling to new places with her husband, Charlie, who has been her constant companion in life's journey. She finds inspiration in everyday moments — quiet mornings, family gatherings, and the lessons found in both joy and hardship.

Jagged Edges: A Journey Through Love, Reflection, and Forgiveness is Shannon's first published collection, bringing together years of personal writings that she hopes will inspire, comfort, and encourage others to embrace their own stories, with all their imperfections, beauty, and grace.